This

Matzah Ball Book

belongs to:

_____

_____

_____

Klutzy   Shmutzy

Kvetchy   Shluffy   Noshy

Kvetchy Boy
Copyright © 2006 by Anne-Marie Asner
Second Printing August 2007
Printed in the United States of America
All rights reserved
www.matzahballbooks.com
Library of Congress Control Number: 2006921643
ISBN-13: 978-0-9753629-3-8
ISBN-10: 0-9753629-3-3

Kvetchy Boy

by Anne-Marie Baila Asner

MATZAH BALL BOOKS®

Kvetchy Boy complains almost all the time and about almost everything.

From the moment he wakes in the morning . . .
"I don't want to get up."

To the moment he goes to bed . . . "I'm not tired."

And many moments in between . . .

"My soup is cold."

"Homework is no fun."

"My friends are late."

Kvetchy Boy always seems to find something to complain about.

Even at his birthday party, Kvetchy Boy kvetched and kvetched.

"The ice cream made my cake soggy. I hate soggy cake," said Kvetchy Boy.

"But Kvetchy Boy," said Noshy Boy, who loves to eat. "The cake tastes even better that way."

Kvetchy Boy didn't agree.

"Somebody gave me a purple shirt. I hate purple,"
said Kvetchy Boy.

"It's my favorite color shirt," said Klutzy Boy, tripping
over his own feet. "I thought you liked mine so I got
you one for a present."

Kvetchy Boy managed to grumble "thank you,"
but he didn't look pleased.

"Shluffy Girl!" shouted Kvetchy Boy. "What's wrong with you? Why are you falling asleep at my party?"

"Kvetchy Boy, your complaining is exhausting me," said Shluffy Girl, sleepy-eyed.

The next day at school, Kvetchy Boy's friends weren't so happy to see him.

Noshy Boy didn't offer to share his snack with Kvetchy Boy.

Klutzy Boy didn't even come near enough to
Kvetchy Boy to stumble over him.

And Shluffy Girl didn't so much as yawn in
Kvetchy Boy's direction.

That day, Kvetchy Boy sat alone at lunch and really had a reason to complain. But no one was there to listen to him.

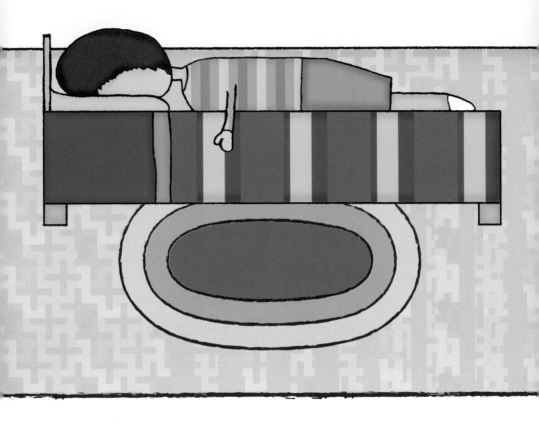

When he got home, Kvetchy Boy went straight to his room.

Bubbe Kvelly, always proud of her grandson, went to see what was the matter.

"Bubbe!" cried Kvetchy Boy. "My friends are mad at me. They say I complain too much."

"Well, Kvetchy Boy, you are quite a kvetcher,"
said Bubbe Kvelly.

"But, Bubbe, there is so much to complain about,"
said Kvetchy Boy.

"Of course there is," said Bubbe Kvelly. "I'm old and have lots of aches and pains, but do you hear me complaining?"

Kvetchy Boy thought for a moment, then he answered, "No, not usually."

"Many things are less than perfect, but if you kvetch all the time, people stop listening. Then when you have something important to complain about no one will help," said Bubbe Kvelly.

When he got to school the next day, Kvetchy Boy told his friends that he would stop kvetching about the little things.

Right away, Noshy Boy offered to share his snack with Kvetchy Boy.

In his excitement, Klutzy Boy knocked over Kvetchy Boy's milk.

And Shluffy Girl sat next to Kvetchy Boy while she napped.

Kvetchy Boy still didn't like getting up in the morning, going to bed at night and many moments in between, but he kept his kvetches to himself.

In return, Kvetchy Boy's friends promised to listen if he ever had something important to complain about. And he knew they would.

Kvetchy   Shluffy   Noshy

Klutzy   Shmutzy

Glossary

A Bissle (little bit) of Yiddish

Bubbe (bŭ-bē) *n.* grandmother

Keppy (kĕpp-ē) *n.* head; *adj.* smart, using one's head

Kibbitzy (kĭbbĭtz-ē) *v. kibbitz* to joke around; *adj. kibbitzy*

Klutzy (klŭts-ē) *adj.* clumsy

Kvelly (k'vĕll-ē) *v. kvell* to be proud, pleased; *adj. kvelly*

Kvetchy (k'vĕtch-ē) *adj.* whiny, complaining

Noshy (nŏsh-ē) *v. nosh* to snack; *adj. noshy*

Shayna Punim (shā-nǎ pŭ-nĭm) *adj.* pretty *(shayna)*; *n.* face *(punim)*

Shleppy (shlĕp-ē) *v. shlep* to carry or drag; *adj. shleppy*

Shluffy (shlŭf-ē) *adj.* sleepy, tired

Shmoozy (shmooz-ē) *adj.* chatty, friendly

Shmutzy (shmŭtz-ē) *adj.* dirty, messy

Tushy (tŭsh-ē) *n.* buttocks, bottom

Zaide (zā-dē) *n.* grandfather

For information about Matzah Ball Books, visit

www.matzahballbooks.com

 **MATZAH BALL BOOKS®** # Products

 **toddler tee**
sizes: 2T & 4T

youth & adult tees ▶
sizes: S, M, L

infant set

Noshy Boy dish set ▶

Shmutzy Girl dish set ▶

HOW TO ORDER:

- website: www.matzahballbooks.com
- e-mail: orders@matzahballbooks.com
- phone: (310) 936-5683